A Duck at the Dog Pound

Written and Illustrated
by

Susann Batson

A Guardian Angel Pets Children's Book

A Duck at the Dog Pound
Copyright © 2006 Susann Batson
Illustrations Copyright © 2006 Susann Batson
ISBN 13: 9781933090443
ISBN 10: 1-933090-44-8
January 2007
First Copyright © 2000 by Susann Batson Bookmice.com, Inc.

Published in the United States of America

GUARDIAN ANGEL PUBLISHING, INC.
12430 Tesson Ferry Road #186
Saint Louis, MO 63128 USA
http://www.guardianangelpublishing.com

A Duck at the Dog Pound

"Quarf! Quarf!" Wiggles shook her long white tail feathers as she practiced her barking that morning.

Wiggles wanted to be a dog. If she was a dog then maybe everyone would love her. She remembered when she was a duckling. The children played with her then and cuddled her all the time.

Wiggles lived in the back yard of the Wallace's house on Christopher Road. She had three playmates: Stanley, Shelby and Sidney. They were Beagle dogs. The four animals played in the backyard and slept inside the cozy dog kennel. Sometimes they went swimming in the small pond at the bottom of the hill.

When Adam and Ashley came home from school each day, they would go for a walk with their mother, taking Stanley, Shelby and Sidney with them. If the children's father came home early, he went too.

But Wiggles wasn't invited. She had to stay home. All by herself.

It seemed like the whole family would be gone for hours on their walks. Wiggles would get very lonely. She'd hop up onto her soft bed and wait.

She sat up a little taller on her bed and took a deep breath. "Quarf!" Well, it was certainly louder. She'd try one more time.

"Quarfff!" Wiggles wings flapped, taking her into the air. Her orange bill bumped against the latch at the gate, opening it. Wiggles landed on the grass outside the kennel.

"Oh dear. This has never happened before. I suppose I should go back inside," Wiggles said.

She started to waddle back where she belonged, but paused. She so longed to go for a walk. If the rest of the family didn't want to take her along, why couldn't she take a walk by herself?

Wiggles waddled across the lush green lawn, feeling quite happy. But when she came to the street her happiness faded. A car roared down the pavement, blaring its' loud horn. "TOOOOT."

Wiggles half waddled, half flew all the way back to the kennel, closing the gate safely behind her.

When Wiggles calmed down from the excitement of leaving the pen, her family returned with the dogs. The dog leashes were put away and the brushes were brought out for grooming. As soon as each Beagle was brushed, Adam took cans of dog food from the cabinet.

It was dinner time. Adam filled the dogs' dishes then patted the top of their heads. He walked past Wiggles, forgetting to pat the top of her head.

Wiggles scurried in front of Adam, bowing her head for a pat of affection. "You forgot about me Adam," quacked Wiggles.

"Oops! Sorry Wiggles." He brushed his fingers along her feathers on his way out the gate.

"Quarf!"

Sidney stopped eating. "Will you cease that awful noise? I've told you no matter what you do; you'll never be a dog."

Tears filled Wiggles' tiny black eyes.

Shelby lifted her head from her bowl. "It's not an awful sound. I think it has character."

Wiggles brightened. Sidney frowned and started to speak.

Stanley interrupted her. "No talking with your mouth full. That's rude."

"Come on over and share my food, Wiggles." Shelby offered. Wiggles scooted in between Sidney and Shelby. Sidney growled with displeasure, but Wiggles ignored her. She was just happy to eat dinner with Shelby.

When they were finished eating, Sidney began bragging to Wiggles about the wonderful walk they had. "Too bad you can't go for walks with us. But ducks can't go for walks."

"Sidney don't be mean," Shelby said.

"I'm taking a nap." Stanley plopped down on the ground and closed his eyes.

"I went for a walk by myself," Wiggles told the dogs.

Shelby wagged her tail excitedly. "All by yourself? Was it fun? Was it scary?"

Stanley lifted one eye lid.

"You must have been dreaming or else you're fibbing." Sidney said.

Shelby came to the rescue. "Wiggles doesn't fib. It's not nice to fib and Wiggles is a nice duck."

Wiggles gasped. "Shelby! You said you would call me a dog!"

"I'm sorry, Wiggles, but if we're going to tell the truth…"

"I know. I'm just a duck." Wiggles bowed her head sadly.

Sidney cleaned her paws, ignoring them.

"How did you get out?" Shelby asked, trying to cheer up her friend.

"Well, we know she didn't fly over the fence." Sidney laughed.

"Wiggles can't help it if flying makes her dizzy." Shelby moved a little closer to Wiggles. "Did you fly? You looked a little green around the edges when we came back from our walk."

"I didn't really fly. It was more of a jump," Wiggles answered.

Stanley opened his other eye.

Sidney howled with laughter. "Of course. Didn't Wiggles tell you she's learning how to be a kangaroo, since she's no good at being a duck or a dog?"

"You jumped over the fence?" Shelby asked in awe.

"No. I guess I have to show you."

"This I have to see," Sidney dared the bird.

Stanley raised his head, his nap forgotten for the moment.

"Oh, do be careful," Shelby whispered.

Wiggles hoped she could open the gate again. She backed up, inhaled deeply and flapped her wings. She tried so hard, a white feather floated into the air. "Quarf!!"

Jumping up, Wiggles snapped at the handle of the gate and watched it open.

Stanley stumbled to his big feet and Sidney dashed out the gate after Wiggles. Shelby nearly passed out.

"Pretty good trick Wiggles," Sidney admitted.

"Thank you." Wiggles ducked her head.

"What should we do now?" Shelby whispered.

"Well, go for a walk of course." Sidney wagged his tail quickly.

"But we're not allowed to go for a walk by ourselves." Shelby said.

"Get back in here before you get us all into trouble." Stanley growled at them.

"Show me where you went for your walk, Wiggles." Sidney encouraged.

"No. I don't want to get you into trouble," Wiggles replied.

"I bet you never went for a walk," Sidney said.

"I did too! And I'll show you," said Wiggles.

Stanley and Shelby hurried after Wiggles and Sidney, afraid to be alone.

In a few minutes they reached Christopher Road. But their outing didn't stop there. Sidney decided to track a rabbit. Before they knew how it happened the other two dogs were following Sidney. Wiggles scurried after them.

They wisely kept to the side of the road, finding safety in the grass.

After arguing with Sidney that she would never find the rabbit, they finally turned to go back home. But before they could reach their yard, the dog catcher trapped them in his net!

The dogs and Wiggles were loaded into the cages of the truck. The dog catcher got behind the steering wheel of the truck and sped off.

Where are we going?" Shelby asked.

To the pound." Stanley answered gruffly.

But I want to go home! The dog pound is a bad place." Shelby howled.

This is all my fault," Wiggles cried.

I'll think of a plan," Sidney said.

No!" the others shouted.

What can we do, Stanley?" Shelby asked.

They won't give you back to your owners if you don't have a collar." Sidney announced.

Wiggles and Shelby cried the rest of the way to the pound. When the friends arrived they were frightened. Even Stanley and Sidney were shaking. The pound was a noisy place. The barking and howling was deafening. The three dogs curled up near each other on the hard concrete floor, keeping Wiggles safe with them.

When they had almost given up hopes of ever seeing the Wallace family again, Mr. and Mrs. Wallace with Adam and Ashley hurried through the door.

Adam came inside the pen. "What happened, Stanley? Father is upset. He has to pay a fine."

"It's my fault," Wiggles explained. "I didn't mean to get everyone into trouble. I just wanted to be a dog."

"Why did you want to be a dog, Wiggles?" Adam asked the duck.

"So that everyone would love me. Then I could go for walks with the family, too."

Adam picked up Wiggles and hugged her. "You don't have to be a dog for us to love you."

Wiggles beamed with happiness.

The next night when it was time to take the family walk, Adam surprised Wiggles with a present. Shelby helped tear the bright paper open. Inside was a small red collar with a matching leash. Adam fastened the collar around Wiggles' neck.

What do her tags say?" Shelby asked.

Wiggles the Duck," Adam said.

Are you taking the duck for a walk?" Sidney asked.

We sure are. She's part of the family, too," replied Adam.

he three dogs barked their pleasure and Wiggles quacked, happy to be a duck!

THE END

Gilly, the Seasick Fish & **A Duck at the Dog Pound** are two award-winning tale of the adventures of a pet goldfish and a duck who wants to be a dog. Your childre will love these charming characters.

Susann Batson is an award winning author/illustrator of enchanting stories full of wisdom and whimsy. Her books are fun to read and inspire a child's imaginatio Susann travels to schools throughout the country presenting programs which is clude writing and illustrating contests and awarding prizes.

Susann owns Angels Princess Tea Party, a business celebrating special occasion with joyful creativity.

She is married to her high school sweetheart. Their four grandbabies from Kim berly and Christopher, and Julie and John, provide her with an endless array of magical story ideas. Susann enjoys hearing from her readers. Look for many mo books written and illustrated by Susann coming soon and published by Guardia Angel Publishing.com

Susann Batson
PO Box 510253
Saint Louis, MO 63151-0253
www.susannbatson.com
susann.batson@sbcglobal.net

Printed in the United States
110218LV00002B